I0760917

WRITTEN BY JEFFREY THOMAS/ALL ARTWORK BY MIKE DUBISCH

SCENES FROM A VILLAGE

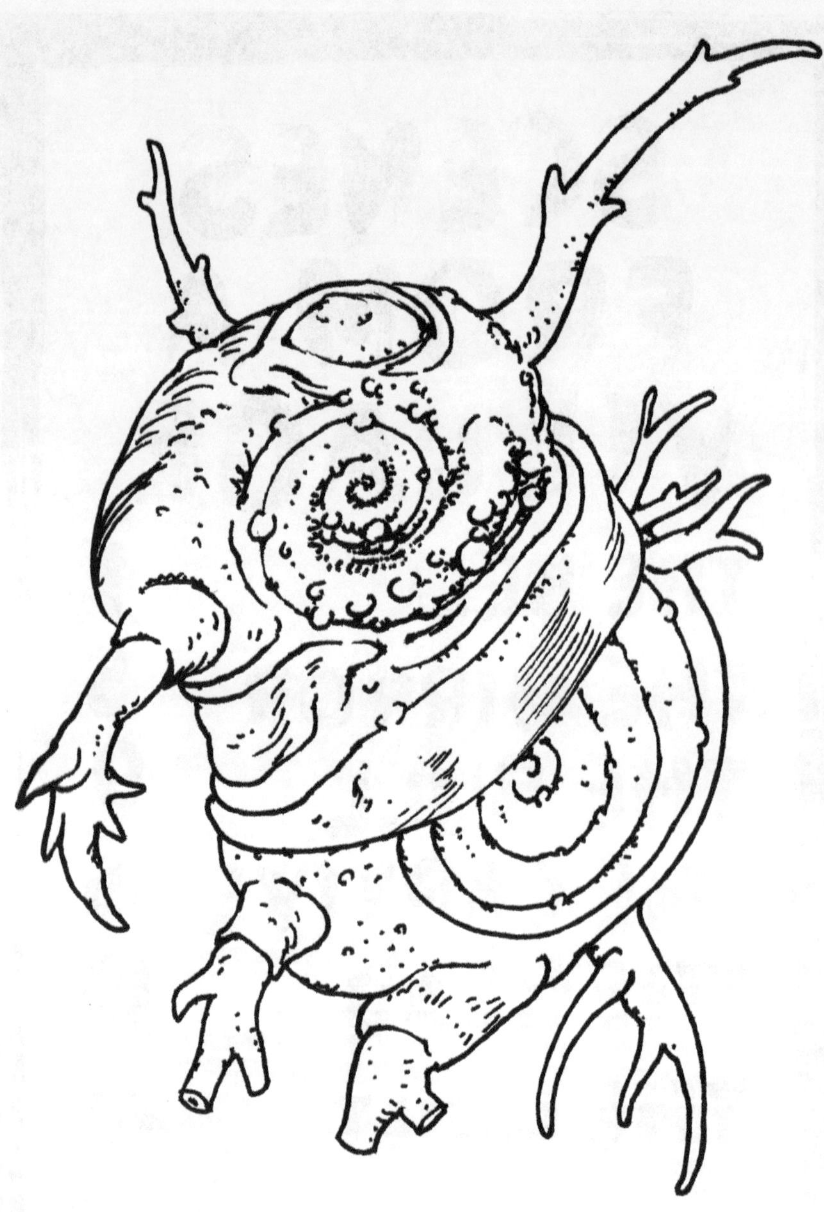

I live in an isolated village, in a green bowl between steep mountains, and with my own eyes I saw the great inverted bell, though you have probably only seen it in videos on the internet.

Atop many of the cell phone masts in my country flies the nation's official flag, which is sewn from transparent silk, so that it unfurls invisible against the sky in day or night, in weather bright or clouded. One *knows* it is there more than one *sees* it is there. If one *doesn't* know, then they are probably a foreign tourist and don't even know we have a flag. The nature of our flag has to do with the name of our country, which translated for Western eyes would read: *The Unnamed Country*. My nation adopted this nameless name, and the conceit of being an invisible country, centuries ago...after many years of efforts from neighboring countries—separated along our most inland border by an intimidating mountain range—to invade and take control of our humble land. Also, the legends say, our great Emperor Tho renamed our country to its nameless state to hide it from the covetous eyes of the demons who were said to have plagued his subjects with bad luck.

That was long before outsiders from Western and Eastern countries alike flew here, over mountains and sea, to help us install cell phone towers. The whole world is linked now by a web as unseen as the flag that we long felt defined us to ourselves and camouflaged us from the world.

Along with those who would help us rear and link up this technology came others: scientists and conservationists who were thrilled to gradually win greater and greater access to our wilder regions—primarily in the dense forests of the aforementioned mountain range and its valleys—to study our flora and fauna, which are often unique to our country, cut off from outer contamination just as we citizens had been for generations.

It came to be, then, that a dismayed team of foreign researchers discovered the negative impact of that imported technology on native species of insect. Mobile phone radiation was affecting the cells of a variety of bees and flies, making them more vulnerable to illness and disrupting their patterns of sleep and wakefulness. The mating call of a certain type of grasshopper had somehow become either distorted or muted, causing their numbers to decline. Most alarmingly, at least to this team, was the pronounced effect on a type of hoverfly found only in my country, said to be sensitive to magnetic fields. This hoverfly, which has evolved to masquerade as a honeybee, is important to the environment in that it is both a pollinator and preys on harmful pests like aphids. Hence the concern. But it was the dramatic manner in which the hoverflies were effected that caused the scientists to ultimately focus on them entirely. And all my fellow villagers, besides.

A cell phone mast loomed on the summit of two almost identical peaks in this forested mountain chain, within sight of each other, radiating their magic. Over time, it was observed that clouds of hoverflies would swam through the air at the exact center point between these twin towers, swirling and dipping and almost seeming to mimic the shape of larger animals like whales, as one sees with birds when they fly in synchronized flocks.

Over time, greater numbers of hoverflies came to be attracted to this spot in the air between the cell phone towers, until one might imagine every hoverfly in the Unnamed Country had been called to join the dance. And now, it not only appeared that their countless bodies were imitating a shape—they *did* form an ultimate shape. For whatever reason, hovering stationary in the air, their many bodies created a shape that some likened to an urn, into which joss sticks might be inserted outside a temple to the Ruby Empress, or a vast inverted bell.

I preferred to think of the hovering black shape in the sky, framed by those tall mountain peaks, as a bell because of the sound it made. The combined humming sound of the wings of those countless linked flies was not loud, exactly, but it was pervasive; it got through your walls. At night, when all other sounds of my village were stilled, it got into your skull. The sound was an itch in my very skin. A god, or a demon, had struck that bell and it seemed its reverberation would go on forever...outlasting our village, and our sanity.

Before the bell finally did dissolve, though—and you have probably seen that process documented in videos—there were further developments, more dramatic still.

As one, all the bodies of the hoverflies began to vibrate, more and more violently. Somehow, miraculously, despite this they were at first able to maintain the bell-like shape. Then, their bodies began to shake apart. Their chitin broke up into shards, and the shards seemed to break up into their individual molecules. The flies liquified, and a black rain fell into the valley between the mountain peaks. Wind blew a mist of this rain across our village, and we hid inside our homes from it. But from our windows, we saw the inverted bell fill up with a black fluid that spilled over its rim and poured through the trees and ran down the mountain flanks into our valley.

Eventually, the inky poison stopped falling, sank into the soil, and the bell dissolved utterly, and now hoverflies are said to have become extinct in the Unnamed Country.

And yet...and yet...in fact, they have migrated to a new environment, from which they won't be expelled. They have simply evolved into a new form. Their atoms, their ghosts, live on inside the heads of the people in my humble village.

Especially in the still of night, I hear their humming. It speaks to me, like a language from someplace far away.

When there had been a war raging in the country that borders ours to one side, the Western enemy dumped great quantities of defoliant from airplanes, to expose guerilla fighters. Fortunately the war never spilled over into our country, but clouds of herbicide did. Though a high and rugged chain of forested mountains forms a natural wall between our two countries, the poison settled onto the peaks, and rains washed it downhill, where it infiltrated the ground water. So it was that our humble village, nestled in one of the mountain valleys, has suffered a good many cases of dramatic birth defects in the decades since that neighboring conflict.

My mother remembers going to school with Phek, and tells me Phek had a beautiful face. Unfortunately, she had another face, too. This one was smaller, with oddly smooth and glossy skin, as if the face of a doll had been sliced off and sewn onto the back of Phek's head. It gazed out through the young girl's long black hair, moving its lips subtly, though no sound was ever heard from it. Everyone said it had no awareness, no thoughts of its own, though my mother points out it blinked its eyes and moved its mouth independently of Phek's movements. Phek tried to hide this lesser developed face with her hair, but wasn't very successful, so she took to wearing a wide colorful headband, in the antiquated way of old mountain women. Still, one could see the features of the secondary face pressing through the material.

One time my mother innocently asked Phek if the other face had its own name, and Phek ran off to her house in tears. Did that mean it did, or it didn't?

A few years later, Phek admitted to my mother she had never seen the second face herself, though others had offered to take a photo of it for her, or help her view it with the use of two mirrors. She said she had no desire to ever set eyes on it.

When she turned seventeen, Phek's parents and the parents of a village boy tried to arrange a marriage. They all thought the boy might agree, because he was born without legs, and because Phek's forward-facing visage was quite attractive. Nevertheless, the boy was horrified by the suggestion. His response was so violent that Phek, always a melancholy girl, was thrown into despair. She was found dead in her home soon after. Before opening the femoral artery in her thigh, she had first reached around to slash at the unseen face of her miniature duplicate.

After the funeral, her ghost began to haunt our village.

At night, Phek's spirit would wander between our little houses, shuffling like a sleepwalker, slowly and silently. No sound came from either her own mouth or that of the miniature face bulging through her long hair at the rear of her skull, though witnesses claimed the lips of both were in constant motion.

My father says he saw her ghost one evening, when a heavy rain started up and he went outside to bring his motorbike into the house. Phek was standing across the road, motionless in the downpour. At least she wasn't looking at him, he said. Phek's head was always tipped downward forlornly, as if she watched only her restless bare feet. Thus, the lesser face was always tilted upward.

My mother saw the specter one time, as well. Come nightfall the fearful villagers always made sure to bolt their doors and shutter their windows, but this night mother went to shutter the windows later than usual, following dinner, and Phek was right outside one window with her face close to the bars. (Our home had no glass panes in any of its windows, which is still common in my village.) My mother cried out Phek's name, but Phek didn't look up to meet her eyes. She just turned away from the window sluggishly and staggered away into the darkness.

A group of our elders hiked up to a roadside temple not far from our village, and begged the monks there to intercede, so that the suffering of villagers and ghost alike might be relieved. Several days later, two of the monks came down the narrow path from the temple to our village carrying a sheet of glass between them. It was of a deep red tint, symbolically like the red glass eyes of Cholukan, the Holy Monkey, which our goddess the Ruby Empress had gifted to him after his eyes were burned out during his adventure in Hell. The monks advised that the sheet of glass should be laid down upon the path that Phek usually took in her nighttime wandering through the village. The glass was blessed, they explained. With her head downcast as always, when Phek chanced upon the red mirror and saw her own reflection in it, she would remember she was dead and be released from her bond to the mortal world.

A spot was chosen, the sheet of red glass was rested on the ground, and the villagers all waited anxiously behind their locked doors and shuttered windows, wondering if Phek would chance upon the mirror that night and if, in gazing upon her own ghost, she would realize she must depart to the spirit realm.

The next morning the people of my village found that their plan had been partly successful. The glass was discovered shattered into fragments, and Phek's tormented spirit was never seen again.

However, on many nights since we have seen a small ball-like shape drifting between our houses. Sometimes it bobs outside our windows, so we are careful to keep them shuttered. I had the misfortune myself, one evening, of curiously peeking outside my house's door and seeing the tiny disembodied head floating there like a hoverfly, its face oddly smooth and glossy, its lips working soundlessly, staring directly into my eyes.

I still don't know if Phek's twin has its own name.

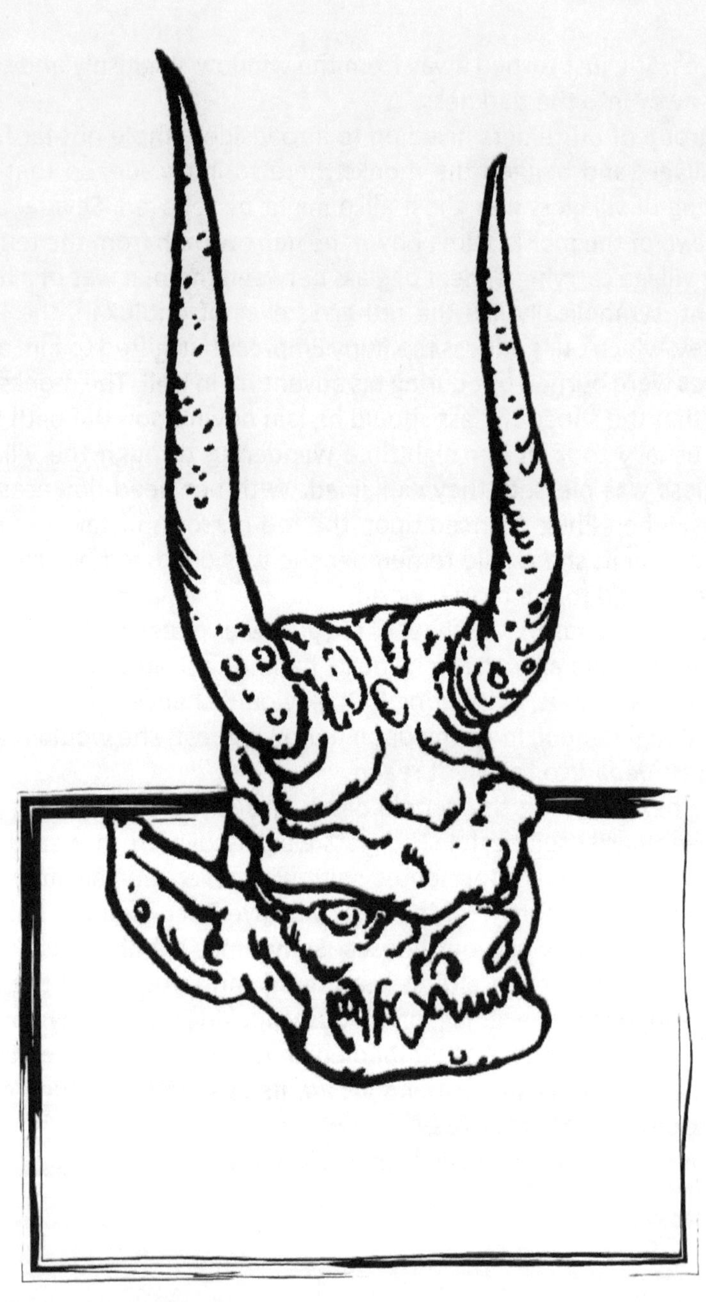

THE BULL

My grandmother seemed to have every adventure of Cholukan memorized by heart, and Cholukan the Holy Monkey had known many an adventure indeed. Cholukan, that yellow-furred macaque, that trickster—the beloved hero of every child in this country of ours. He was scribe to the Gods, sent to Earth by his mistress the Ruby Empress to report back firsthand on the doings of mortals, yet Cholukan unwisely journeyed into Hell to rescue a kidnapped human girl he loved, who did not love him in return—a quest that cost him his eyes, burnt up in their sockets. But the glorious goddess, the Ruby Empress, loved her pet so dearly that she mercifully restored his vision with new eyes of red glass, formed from her own tears of blood, and she returned him to Earth to continue wandering and recording his fantastical experiences.

One evening, as a young boy, I groused at the dinner table that the scraps of beef laid atop my steamed rice were too scanty. My father snapped at me that beef does not grow in rice paddies, and I resumed chewing in silence. My grandmother said nothing to defend either my father or myself, but took note of my sullenness, and that night at my bedside told me this story.

There was once a rural temple of corrupt monks who behind their sheltering wall played cards, drank gallons of rice wine, entertained unchaste women, and who exacted excessive tributes of money from the local villagers. An earthquake struck that region, a great sinkhole opened beneath the temple, and it was swallowed in the deep pit—with every monk killed. No doubt, an act of divine retribution. However, a group of demons took advantage of the situation, this rift between the Earth and the netherworld, and escaped up into the mortal realm. But, their success was not as they imagined it.

In Hell, this particular race of demons was composed of fearsome warriors with muscled human-like bodies and the heads of bulls, long glossy horns curving out from their skulls. Upon entering the mortal world, though, they could not retain their infernal form, or infernal nature. Instantly, every one of them was changed into a mute, simpleminded, and docile four-legged beast...and thus, there came about the yellow breed of cattle we know in our country today.

We are in general not a prosperous country, grazing land is limited, and so cattle are not as plentiful as abroad. Thus, beef can be pricey for many families. Chicken, pork, goat, and seafood are much more accessible. Even when our country was less thickly settled, generations ago, this was the case.

One old man whom Cholukan encountered in his travels had what he considered a clever solution to this problem. In his younger days this individual had been an officer in the army, and as such had been spoiled with beef, and to his proud mind nothing less would suffice. He owned, though, just a single old bull, haggard and subdued. Cholukan saw it standing in a scrap of field, nibbling at little tufts of grass, and stopped to gaze upon it. Seeing him there, the old soldier emerged from his humble home to approach him. He limped along with the aid of a cane, as quickly as he could.

"It is you," said the veteran, "the Holy Monkey I have heard of, the scribe of the Gods! Welcome, I am honored! Have you heard of me, as well? Have you come to record my deeds, my battles against invading armies, so as to recount my exploits to your lords?"

Cholukan had no idea who the man was, however, until he was told. Instead, he pointed toward the lone bull with the walking stick he always carried, which he also used as a flute and a fighting staff. "That animal there," he said. "I have a strange feeling when I look upon it. Why is it so scarred? Was it maimed by these invading forces you mention?"

The veteran laughed. “Ah! I can’t afford more than the one beast now, in this ungrateful country. I am forced to strip thin slices of meat from this creature occasionally...not enough to weaken it unto death, of course. My nephews help me control it at such times, as I am not the strong bull I once was...ha ha!”

“You...take flesh from this live animal to eat?”

“I do...clever, eh? But I must give it time to heal, so I can’t be too greedy. At other times, instead, I poke a lance into its neck to drain its blood into a vessel. A little plaster on the wound, a period of healing, and the source of my nourishment is waiting for me next time, like a bottle of wine that magically refills itself!”

“It seems a cruel fate to be tortured thus, endlessly.”

“Cruel?” the old man barked at Cholukan. “It is still alive, is it not? But where are my parents, where is my wife, where are my brothers now? All dead, while this animal lives on, blissful in its ignorance! Grass in its belly, warm sun on its skin. What *would* be cruel is letting this old soldier starve to death! If my country won’t provide for me, I must provide for myself as I may!”

And with that, the veteran snorted angrily and retreated to his home, limping from some old wound of his own, slamming his door behind him.

Cholukan thought to return to his path, but glanced at the bull again, and he saw it watching him. This time, with the old man gone, he heard in his brain the voice he had only faintly sensed before.

“Monkey,” called the bull’s voice in his head, and Cholukan entered the field to draw close to the creature.

“How do you speak to me?” Cholukan asked.

“I was once the captain of a squad of demons who foolishly escaped into this world from Hell...just as you yourself once foolishly ventured *into* Hell. I suffer such indignities here, I wish I had remained where I was! I wait for the day my human master can’t restrain himself, and kills me for my steaks...or at least, I pray he will accidently open the vein in my throat too deeply.”

“Your situation brings me pain, demon.”

“Would you, then, take pity upon me and dispatch me yourself, so that I might find the nonexistence I crave? Free of afterworld and mortal world alike?”

Cholukan’s brow furrowed at this dilemma. “I have killed demons before, and plenty, but only in battle. This situation is another matter—a human matter, as your master is a mortal man—and I’m not sure I can intercede.”

"I beg you! Can you at least relate my woes to your mistress, the Ruby Empress, and ask her to take pity on me in some way?"

"I fear I can only inscribe all this in my records, which of course will be laid before the goddess's eyes."

Just then, from behind him, Cholukan heard the old soldier cry out, "You there! Trickster monkey! What are you doing with my animal? You intend to free him and take him off with you, don't you? Get away from him this instant!"

Cowed, the bull put its forlorn head down nervously and resumed nibbling at the sparse grass before it.

Cholukan stepped back as the old man came limping at him furiously. He raised his stick above his head, as if he even meant to strike the Holy Monkey, scribe to the Gods or no. "Just a dirty animal!" he raged, though Cholukan wondered if he meant himself or the bull.

But in his anger, and in his momentum, the old man lost his balance and pitched forward. In so doing, he impaled his face on one of the bull's long, curved horns. The horn pierced him under the jaw, so that its end emerged from his mouth. The bull raised its head in surprise, in so doing lifting the veteran a ways from the ground.

Thus pinned, the frail old soldier stared up at Cholukan, unable to speak, but his agonized eyes seemed to beg the monkey to free him.

"I'm afraid I can't intercede in this matter between the two of you," Cholukan said to the former soldier, having squatted down beside him. "But I offer you these words of comfort, sir...at least you are still alive!"

Having said this, Cholukan met the bull's eyes, cocked back the walking stick he also used as a flute and fighting staff, and struck the bull smartly upon the hindquarters...sending it into a gallop away from the old man's field, dragging its master with it.

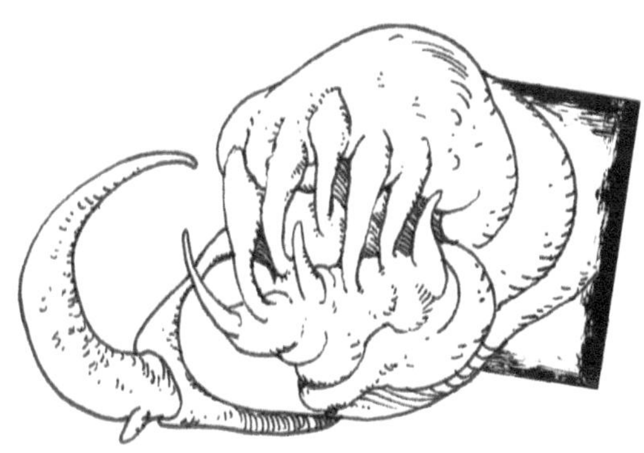

My village—tucked as it is in a crease between the imposing tree-furred mountains that separate our country from the neighbor with whom we share the longest border—is one of the remotest in the land. Our country has been so cut off from the rest of the world for so many years (and not accidentally, though that has gradually changed with time) that outsiders are just as ignorant of much of our animal life as those animals are of them. What wildlife these Western outsiders and others do learn of, they marvel at. And there are some creatures that for them remain only rumor, because we hardly know of them ourselves.

My own people have often dismissed stories that in the isolated mountain forests and deepest tropical jungles, there lives a type of Wildman, known by several names depending on the region, said to be covered in yellowish fur. Its yellow fur and ape-like appearance are the reasons one nickname for the being would translate to Westerners as "Son of Cholukan," Cholukan of course being the Monkey God, the scribe to the Gods. Many in my country would sooner believe that the Cholukan of folklore truly existed before believing in the Wildman. Ah, but these people, perhaps dwelling in Westernized cities like Haikan, don't live where I live. They would scoff and say the Wildman accounts can be attributed to sightings of monkeys or apes...as if rural folk who know monkeys and apes couldn't tell the difference.

As a child, I got chills whenever my Uncle Buom related an experience from his own childhood. He and two chums had ventured up a mountainside, looking for a good spot to turn into a secret play fort, when they spied a figure further up the cliff face, observing their slow ascent. The figure was smallish, as the Wildmen are said to be, only as tall as Buom's mother. Naked, covered in yellowish-red fur, with a leathery face and what my uncle described as dark, intelligent eyes. Yes, he saw it from a distance, but he swore he discerned that quality. When the Wildman saw that it had been noticed it straightened up alertly, and when the boys pointed at it and cried out, the creature swiftly turned, clambered up the cliff, and vanished amongst the trees.

The most famous story of all about my country's Wildman is one which even Westerners discuss now, some wanting to believe in it, others mocking it. Perhaps you have seen videos about the case online.

Over one hundred-and-fifty years ago, hunters brought back to their village a strange being they had captured alive and tightly bound, having suffered a few nasty bites in the process. It was something between human and ape, a female, less than five feet in height, head to toe covered in shaggy blondish hair. Drawings of her show a bony brow, wide flat nostrils, a heavy jutting jaw, and narrow eyes glittering black. She was caged, and—as word of her spread—displayed to many who traveled just to see her. Soon, her captors brought her to *them*, and charged the curious for the opportunity to view her. In time, she became tame, or perhaps just resigned. To make her public appearances more entertaining, her captors started dressing her in human clothing, embroidered silken robes and such, like a woman of distinction. They had by now given her a name: Luwon.

That there was an odd beauty (one might even say a dignity) in Luwon's face, as portrayed in those old drawings and paintings, might not have had anything to do with her becoming pregnant. Perhaps the man who got her that way, one of her captors, had only been drunk and feeling perverse. Perhaps it was in the spirit of his mastery over her. He was known, after all, to beat her severely, even in front of his paying customers. Unless he harbored some different feelings for her that he hid from others, maybe even denied to himself.

Unfortunately, Luwon died in childbirth, at an unknown age, though apparently quite young.

Her captors mourned the loss, and left the body to he who had fathered her child. But rather than bury or cremate his unlikely bride, he could not bring himself to stop exhibiting her. He had Luwon crudely mummified, and placed into a coffin with a glass lid...though those who viewed her in later years said her face looked to be more of painted plaster than anything else. In drawings of Luwon in this state, her dark eyes stare through the glass in something like uncomprehending despair.

The child, a boy his father chose to name Phip—as the mother never learned to speak—was said to look almost completely like a typical human. His father didn't let this stop him, however, from exhibiting the boy alongside his dead mother, billing him as the "Progeny of Cholukan." Phip was dressed like Cholukan in a blue silk robe, given a miniature walking stick like Cholukan's (which also served as flute and fighting staff), and taught to jump about and laugh uproariously in the manner of the Monkey God.

But the boy never actually learned to speak, either. And his father beat him often, as he had beat Luwon. He drank heavily, often passed out from his drinking. Phip reached the age of eight.

One night, terrible shrieks were heard from the man's home and neighbors rushed to see what the matter was. Inside, they found the father of Phip dead on the floor of his bedroom, blood splattered and sprayed everywhere. The man's throat had been ripped open, as if by the teeth of a wild animal.

Though bloody bare footprints led the way to the home's open door, the boy Phip was never found. Some say he disappeared into the forest. Some say he lived his life among men.

Whatever his fate, the merciful monks of the local temple took it upon themselves to burn the preserved body of Luwon, the Wildwoman.

hen I turned thirteen, my father took me with him on an arduous hike high into the mountains, in a valley of which our village reposes—higher than I have ever been before or since. We set out before the sun had even risen, carrying food my mother packed for us. Sometimes we followed narrow but well-worn paths that wound up through the forest, at other times we had to clamber over bare rock. Sometimes boulders were marked for hikers like us with a painted symbol. This symbol, in yellow paint, always showed the outline of a human head.

Along the easier paths, when we weren't huffing with exertion, my father would tell me more about our mission and destination. His father had brought him on this same journey when he himself had turned thirteen (then two years later my grandfather had taken my uncle). It was not required, but common for the folk of our village to bring their sons to give thanks to a great monk named Vheng Jhi.

Vheng Jhi had originally been a monk at a little monastery nearer to our village, a roadside temple with a lovely statue of the Ruby Empress outside, a popular stop these days for foreign tourists on their way from one scenic site to another. However, Vheng Jhi and a female monk had fallen in love, and he had impregnated her, so she had left the temple in disgrace. The story is that when her son was born, a long needle was inserted into its head so as to send its blighted soul back into the ether. To repent, Vheng Jhi himself began constructing a smaller, less accessible temple higher in the mountains. A few other monks, each of them also chastened for some failing or another, joined him to complete the temple and dwell there with him.

Many years later, women in my village would dream of Vheng Jhi. They always described seeing his bald head floating toward them across the tranquil green sea that bears us along in sleep. The head would finally hover directly in front of them, its eyes peacefully closed but its lips moving as though uttering silent prayers. Any woman who dreamed this vision would soon find herself to be pregnant, and her child would always be a son. My father revealed to my astonished self that my own mother had experienced this dream, before my parents realized she was with child.

Over the decades, the contrite young monk had become increasingly devout, so intent on proving his devotion that he would fast almost to the point of death, or tattoo long prayers into the skin of his legs until they were almost black with logographs. In his efforts to prove to himself, and to inspire his fellow monks, that the spirit far outweighs the value of sinful, limiting flesh, he sliced off all his toes, one by one, over a course of ten days. He bore the pain without complaint, and his healing was said to be extraordinary. Because of this, he was finally able to coax two of his fellows to chop off his feet with an axe. Again, he sat impassively through the ordeal, and survived without bleeding to death or suffering infection.

A year later, he exhorted the other monks to chop off his legs below the knees. This was done. The flesh from the tops and soles of his feet had already been preserved, and now more flesh was unrolled from the shins and calves of his severed legs, and all this skin was dried out to form the pages of a book. The covers of the book were created from thick patches of flesh that Vheng Jhi himself carved from his breasts. The book was bound, and Vheng Jhi inked prayers into its pages.

One day, my father related, from inside Vheng Jhi's room the other monks heard a strange thunk, and the rolling of an object upon the floor. They looked in to find the youngest of their number weeping, standing over Vheng Jhi's decapitated body with a sword in his hands. At first the others seized him, believing him to have murdered their master, but the sobbing monk insisted that the master had commanded him to perform this deed.

The eldest of the remaining monks scooped up Vheng Jhi's head, now weeping himself, and cradled it in his arms. It was while holding the head this way that the eldest monk felt the head's lips moving, brushing the skin of his bare chest.

The other monks gathered around and marveled at this miracle. Though Vheng Jhi's eyes were closed, his mouth was indeed moving. He had no vocal cords with which to actually produce sound, but the monks determined by reading his lips that their master was reciting prayers, over and over.

Word trickled down to our village, and from there to other villages, and thereafter pilgrims would find their way up to the remote temple founded by Vheng Jhi to ask for his blessings, or simply to pray to him in tribute, or simply to view his miraculous living head, which had been placed upon a cushion on the altar. It was at this time that dreams had begun coming to expectant mothers. It developed that fathers journeyed to the temple to thank the saintly monk for their sons, in the hope that they too would sire healthy heirs.

Oiled in sweat, my father and I finally arrived at the temple. We left our sneakers outside, and entered the incense-thick gloom. Candles burned upon the altar. At its base were offerings of fruit and flowers, and there was a box for donations to the temple. A very old monk seated nearby, frail in his sapphire blue robes, nodded at us with a gentle smile when we each slipped a note into the donations box. (My father whispered to me that this was said to be the young monk who had severed the master's head.) We lit joss sticks and stood before the altar, thinking inward prayers. We placed the joss sticks into a sand-filled urn, and then stepped up to view Vheng Jhi more closely. My father went first, murmured something, and then moved aside to watch as I approached the head.

Decades since Vheng Jhi's decapitation, the skin of his face was as dark and leathery as the tough pages of the prayer book that rested atop the altar beside him. The green silk cushion the head rested upon was changed every year, and in the candlelight it shimmered like the waters of the ocean of dream. And though the lids of Vheng Jhi's eyes were closed and almost fused with his cheeks, when I bravely leaned in close I could make out that his blackened lips—shriveled and stretched back from his brown teeth—were almost imperceptibly, but unmistakably, moving.

I remember this story today because this morning my girlfriend, Buyen, told me of a dream she had last night...

After she had related this dream to me, I asked her to be my wife.

I love to listen to my girlfriend Buyen tell bedtime stories to her nieces and nephews, and my nieces and nephews when she visits my family, because it's easy to imagine her telling these stories to our own forthcoming child. She's very good at it, makes them stop giggling and elbowing each other to really listen, eyes wide, and she seems to know fables and folklore I've never heard of before, such as some especially strange adventures of Cholukan, the Monkey God, scribe to the gods and their agent on the earthly plane. Well, to be fair, Cholukan certainly has had a lot of strange adventures, more than any one mortal could know.

Tonight, because Buyen's sister's rambunctious twin boys had been fussing about going to bed on time, Buyen ordered them into their room, sat on the edge of their floor mattress (I sat on a plastic stool in the corner, trying to be as inconspicuous as the gecko stuck to the wall near the ceiling), and she told them to pull their quilt up tight to their necks and whatever they did, they must not risk peeking beneath it again until morning...even if they heard a strange tinkling sound down near their feet.

Once, Buyen told the brothers, Cholukan was walking from one adventure to another adventure when his path took him through a deep forest, much like the forest that surrounds our humble village today in its fold between mist-crested mountains. Evening was near and Cholukan felt he must camp amongst the trees, not knowing of any settlements nearby. Just as he was leaning his walking staff against a trunk and slinging off his pack, he heard a musical tinkling sound approaching. The Holy Monkey looked up and saw a ghastly figure come bursting from the underbrush. It was a demon, somehow escaped from Hell; but these things happened sometimes. She had the slim and graceful body of a human woman, entirely unclothed except for anklets made of tiny gold bells. For a head, however, she possessed only a mirror in an oval gold frame. When the demon spotted Cholukan, she turned her mirror face anxiously back the way she had come, to see if she were being pursued. Then, determining she had time to explain her situation to Cholukan, she took a few steps toward him. In a voice like that of a mortal woman but sounding weirdly distant, the demon related her story.

The young and handsome son of a local feudal lord had been interviewing women to be his bride, but he had deemed none of them worthy of his station and much-lauded beauty. He had brusquely rejected one after another. Then, today he had been hunting boar with some of his men when he had heard a lovely, beguiling tinkling sound and followed it, coming upon this escaped demon, cowering behind a bush. He had knelt down and parted the leaves that hid her, revealing a sensuous body of smooth young flesh, topped by the most exquisite face he had ever set eyes on, a face that complemented his own beauty to an astonishing degree. Immediately, he had known that this strange woman must be a gift from the gods and therefore must become his bride. He professed his love for the mysterious woman on the spot, but without a word she bolted off into the forest. The young man tore after her, leaving his men calling behind him in confusion.

The demon ran for all she was worth, frightened now by this mortal's fervor, forgetting the demons who had been hunting her so as to return her to Hell, these other demons being in the guise of wild pigs so that they would not be recognized by humans. It was these demon overlords who had locked the strings of bells on her ankles, having previously suspected she would attempt such an escape.

But these bells were what enabled the young man to continue chasing after her. She splashed through streams, panted up slopes, plummeted down their other sides, and here she was now...wondering if she had thrown the obsessed young man off her track at last.

Yet just then, Cholukan and the demon both heard the call of the feudal lord's son, begging her to stop fleeing, promising he would devote himself to her happiness forever.

The demon admitted to Cholukan then that it had been a mistake coming to the mortal world, because with her bizarre form she could never blend in. She further admitted that she hadn't come here because of her affection for human beings, but because she was addicted to their flavor. In Hell, she and her sisters would dismember the damned limb by limb and feed their parts into the liquid mirrors of their faces, until such time as the damned regenerated and could be dismembered again. She so savored the taste of their souls that she had been driven mad wondering what living humans would taste like.

The voice of her would-be suitor grew louder, and the demon gave Cholukan a polite nod and plunged away into the forest again. Only moments later, a handsome young man emerged from the underbrush where the demon had first appeared. Huffing, he asked Cholukan which way the gorgeous young woman he had been pursuing had fled, and the Holy Monkey only shrugged innocently. But then they both detected the distant tinkling bells, and the lord's son grinned. He said it was meant to be that she should be headed in that direction, for there lay the little cabin he and his men frequently used when hunting boar. Surely she would attempt hiding therein! So off the young man ran, and too curious to resist, Cholukan retrieved his pack and walking staff and followed after both of them.

Soon Cholukan came upon a sturdy wooden cabin built in a clearing, and he saw its door stood open. He stole inside quietly, and from a gloomy back room he heard several odd muffled sounds. One was a subtle crystalline tinkling, and the other a wet slurping, like boots tramping through sucking mud.

Cholukan poked his head into this room, which held a raised wooden platform to be used as a bed. Upon this base was an old, thick quilt sewn together from squares of metallic gold silk. This quilt was oddly humped from the two bodies hidden underneath it. As Cholukan watched, and listened to the shifting sounds of tiny bells, gradually those two bodies beneath the quilt became one.

At last, the demon poked out her oval face of hungry liquid glass, and she courteously informed the Holy Monkey that she was done with the cabin, and she would now leave in search of her pig-demon masters, if he cared to make use of the cabin himself tonight.

Cholukan thanked the demon for her offer, but told her he would rather not, and he turned away to camp in the forest as he had intended.

Buyen had finished her bedtime story, and stared at the naughty brothers sternly, and I couldn't help but laugh aloud when one of the boys said to her, "Auntie, you expect us to sleep after *that?*"

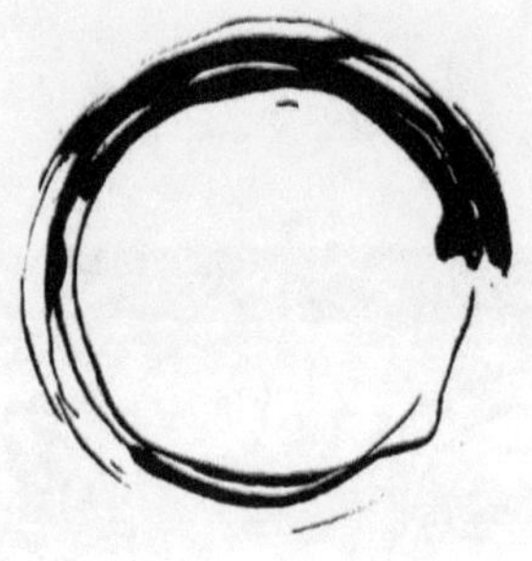

This book is dedicated to the memory of my niece, Truong Thi Thanh Thuy. —JET

JEFFREY THOMAS

The author of such horror and science fiction novels as THE AMERICAN, DEADSTOCK (finalist for the John W. Campbell Award), BLUE WAR, MONSTROCITY (finalist for the Bram Stoker Award), LETTERS FROM HADES, SUBJECT 11, and BONELAND. His short story collections include PUNKTOWN, GHOSTS OF PUNKTOWN, THE UNNAMED COUNTRY, HAUNTED WORLDS, UNHOLY DIMENSIONS, THIRTEEN SPECIMENS, and THE ENDLESS FALL. Stories by Thomas have been reprinted in THE YEAR'S BEST FANTASY AND HORROR, THE YEAR'S BEST HORROR STORIES, and YEAR'S BEST WEIRD FICTION. Though he considers Vietnam his second home, he resides in Massachusetts.

Take Your Choice of His Best Books

PUNKTOWN - *In the nightmarish city they call Punktown, on a planet where countless sentient species collide, you can become a creator of clones. You can become a piece of performance art. You might even become a library of sorrows...*

LETTERS FROM HADES - *A travelogue of Hell—a world not that far from the very world we live in now. It is a story of rebellion, a story of love and a story of hope and rebirth set in a beautifully dark and textured world.*

THE AMERICAN - *Former US tunnel rat Richard Trenor - disfigured in the war, but left with strange gifts as a result - is summoned back to Vietnam by Thanh, the son of an old friend, to find the man who killed Thanh's eight-year-old sister.*

CARRION MEN - *Horror fiction is meant to push boundaries, to shake up expectations, to travel into realms of the taboo and strange. In Carrion Men, you will find tales of sexual anomaly, disturbing mutations of the body, tales of loneliness and isolation.*

THE UNNAMED COUNTRY - *A mosaic novel weaving tales of a land and people poised between the ancient traditions of the past and the burgeoning technology of the future. Where devils, gods, and ghosts still haunt the land, and where you may just discover a unicorn.*

And Many More Choices Available Online

www.ingramcontent.com/pod-product-compliance
Lightning Source LLC
Chambersburg PA
CBHW020325030826
48979CB00020B/53

* 9 7 8 1 9 6 0 2 1 3 0 1 3 *